THIS IS A BORZOI BOOK PUBLISHED BY ALFRED A. KNOPF ● Copyright © 2005 by
Lynn Rowe Reed ● All rights reserved under International and
Pan-American Copyright Conventions. Published in the United States by
Alfred A. Knopf, an imprint of Random House Children's Books, a division
of Random House, Inc., New York, and simultaneously in Canada by Random
House of Canada Limited, Toronto. Distributed by Random House, Inc.,
New York. ● KNOPF, BORZOI BOOKS, and the colophon are registered
trademarks of Random House, Inc. ● www.randomhouse.com/kids ● Library
of Congress Cataloging-in-Publication Data ● Reed, Lynn Rowe.
Thelonius Turkey lives! : (on Felicia Ferguson's farm) / Lynn Rowe Reed. —
1st ed. ● p. cm. ● SUMMARY: As Thanksgiving Day approaches, Thelonius
Turkey becomes worried when Felicia the farmer starts to fatten him
up and pluck his feathers. ● ISBN 0-375-83126-6 (trade) —
ISBN 0-375-93126-0 (lib. bdg.) [1. Turkeys—Fiction. 2. Thanksgiving
Day—Fiction. 3. Domestic animals—Fiction. 4. Farms—Fiction.] I. Title.
● PZ7.R25273The 2005 [E]—dc22 2005003821 ●
MANUFACTURED IN CHINA ● September 2005 ●
10 9 8 7 6 5 4 3 2 1 ● First Edition

the artist's HAND

wobble

THANKS,
JUDY STUART.
XO

Every year,

a plump, wattle-y turkey

disappeared just before

Thanksgiving

gobble

This year, there was only

1 turkey

left on Felicia Ferguson's farm.

NOVEMBER

It was just a week before Thanksgiving, and THELONIUS TURKEY was becoming nervous about dinner—

being dinner,

that is.

Every day, Felicia fed Thelonius three SQUARE meals of special seeds. Then she plucked feathers from him and put them in a big bag.

Thelonius thought that Felicia was trying to fatten him up for the chopping block and was plucking his feathers to better see his size.

GULP

He was becoming very SCARED.

With just seven days until Thanksgiving, Thelonius Turkey gathered his farm friends and made an announcement.

"I will _not_ go to the chopping block without a fight.

Ferocious Felicia's GOTTA GO!"

The next day, Thelonius got to work.
He was up bright and early, doing a little
plumbing while everyone slept. Cow helped.

When Felicia
showered that
morning, she was
udderly
surprised!

milk

On the fifth day before
Thanksgiving, Thelonius found
a can of paint in the barn and
made a beautiful sign.

All of the geese knew
how to read.

gobble

Still, Felicia was friendly.
She kept feeding Thelonius
and plucking his feathers.

"Lovely day, Thelonius,"
she said.
"Not if you're a fat
turkey," he gobbled.

WiSH BONe

You get one wish with a wishbone.
Thelonius wished he could
stay alive.

Imagining the worst made Thelonius a very _naughty_ turkey.

The pigs disappeared one day. Felicia looked for them everywhere.

under the tractor

in the pond

in the haystack

in the trash can

She searched until she was so
exhausted that she needed a nap.

PEE-U!

ZZZZZZZ

Then, just three days before Thanksgiving, Thelonius cooked up another bright IDEA-

3 DAYS

hard-boiled eggs
for the chickens to lay!

CLOMP
CLOMP

On the second day before Thanksgiving—the day before the chopping block—Thelonius was busy playing all kinds of tricks.

That evening, he came up with a plan. If Felicia overslept the next morning, she wouldn't get him to the chopping block on time.

He would _have_ to keep her awake. A good thunderstorm would work. Felicia hardly slept a wink.

tick tick tick

Still, Felicia woke up the next morning with
a spring in her step.
"I have a surprise for you," she told
Thelonius. "I'd like to show you the new
block in town."

"Ha! You mean the chopping
block," gobbled Thelonius
with a groan.

So Felicia loaded
Thelonius in the
pickup truck and
drove toward town.

HISS

THUNK

WHIRR

Sounds CLANKED and WHIRRED
from the building where they parked.
Felicia grabbed Thelonius by the neck.
Thelonius was so scared, even his wattle

shook.

They went inside.

"Well, I'll be stuffed!" proclaimed Thelonius.

"I'm a hat entrepreneur. A fashion phenom! The guru of GORGEOUS!"

On Thanksgiving Day,
Thelonius fixed a feast
fit for Felicia.

"Lovely dinner," said Felicia.
"Lovely day," replied Thelonius.

Giving

Felicia, Thelonius, and
all of his friends
stuffed
themselves.
And they all gave
thanks.

Today,
Thelonius Turkey
still lives on the farm
with all of his

friends...

Africa

North America

England

Mexico

. . . and on the heads of people

all over the world.

France

Brazil

australia

Thelonius Feather Cookies

Ingredients:
(Cookies)
2 ¾ cups flour
¼ teaspoon salt
12 tablespoons butter, softened
¾ cup sugar
1 egg
1 teaspoon vanilla
1 tablespoon lemon zest (optional)

(Decoration)
2 egg yolks
Assorted food coloring

Equipment:
Feather-shaped cookie cutter
   (a narrow leaf or oval shape will work)
Large bowl
Assorted measuring cups and spoons
Small art brushes
Electric mixer
Cookie sheet
Rolling pin
5 small dishes

Directions:
Cream the butter until soft in a large bowl with an electric mixer. Gradually add the sugar and continue beating until light and fluffy. Add the egg, vanilla, and lemon zest (optional) and mix well. Blend the flour and salt and gently stir into the butter to make a dough. Divide the dough into thirds and wrap each piece in plastic wrap. Refrigerate for about 30 minutes to make the dough easier to handle. Preheat the oven to 350 degrees. On a floured surface, roll out the dough to about $\frac{1}{8}$ inch thick. (Thicker cookies will be softer, thinner cookies more crispy.) Then stamp out feathers with your cookie cutter and gently place the cookies on a cookie sheet.

To make colorful feathers, you can paint the cookies with edible colors before baking. To make edible paints, blend 2 egg yolks together and then divide the liquid into 5 small dishes. Add ½ teaspoon yellow food coloring to make yellow paint, ½ teaspoon red for red, ¼ teaspoon for green, ¼ teaspoon for blue, and a combination of 1 ½ teaspoons red, 1 ½ teaspoons green, and 5 drops blue to make black. Use small, clean art brushes to paint the cookies and then bake.

Bake until very lightly colored, about 8–12 minutes. Then transfer to a wire rack and let them cool. Gobble them up!

ALWAYS get a grown-up to help

"Life Is Sweet" Potatoes with Marshmallow Casserole

Ingredients:

8 sweet potatoes
½ stick butter, softened
4 tablespoons sugar
½ teaspoon cinnamon
¼ teaspoon nutmeg
¼ cup orange juice
1 tablespoon vanilla
1 bag marshmallows

Equipment:

Large bowl
Large fork or masher
Assorted measuring cups
  and spoons
9" x 12" casserole dish,
  lightly greased

Directions:

Poke holes in the potatoes with a fork. Cook the potatoes in the microwave until they are soft—about 15 minutes at high power. Preheat oven to 350 degrees. Let the potatoes cool down enough to handle them, then peel the skins off with your fingers and throw them away. Put the potatoes and the butter in a bowl and mash them with a large fork or masher. They should be soft and smooth. Add the sugar, cinnamon, nutmeg, orange juice, and vanilla and mix thoroughly. Pour the mixture into a lightly greased casserole dish. Cover the top with marshmallows—the more, the better! Bake about 10–15 minutes, until the potatoes are hot and the marshmallows melt and become toasty. Enjoy!